ODD DOG OUT

For Mum and Dad

First published in hardback in Great Britain by HarperCollins Children's Books in 2016

10 9 8 7 6 5 4 3 2 1

ISBN: 978-0-00-759415-3

HarperCollins Children's Books is a division of HarperCollins Publishers Ltd.
Text and illustrations copyright © Rob Biddulph 2016

Visit our website at www.harpercollins.co.uk

Printed and bound in China

ODD DOG OUT

Written and illustrated by

Rob Biddulph

HarperCollins *Children's Books*

For busy dogs
a busy day,

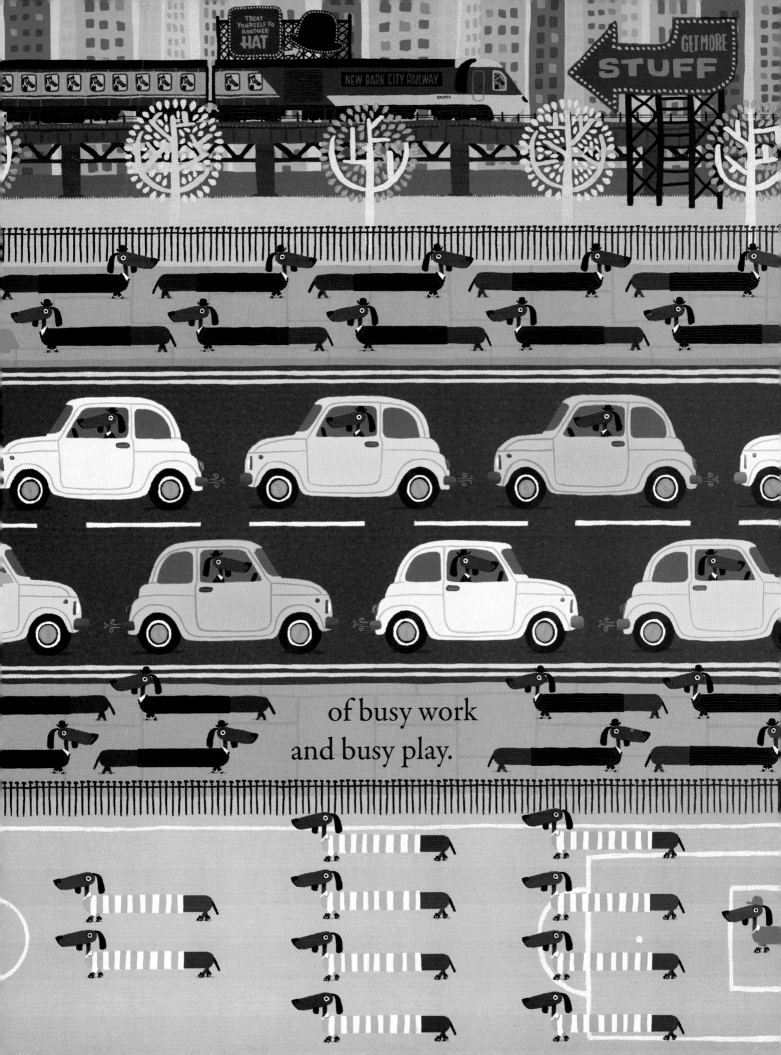

of busy work
and busy play.

Swimmer...

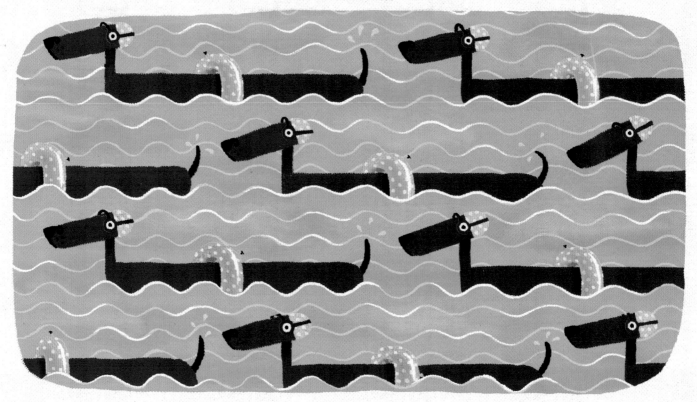

Sailor...

Soldier...

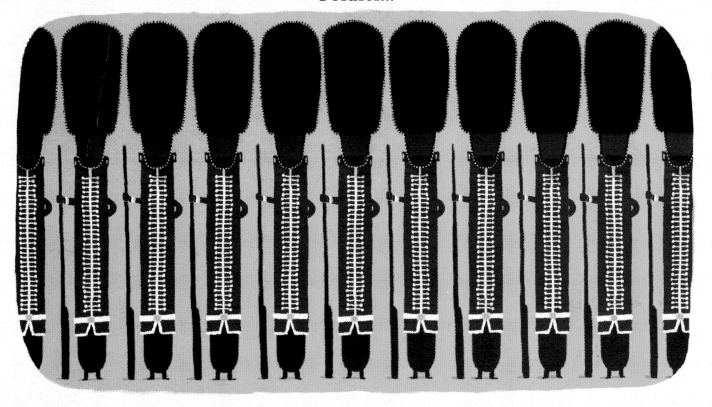

Scout...

They all blend in. No dog stands out.

But wait. Look closer. Can you see
One dog behaving differently?

Someone on this
busy street

Is dancing to a
different beat.

When they fly high...

...this dog flies low.

When they say "Kick!"...

...this dog says "Throw!"

It's very sad
(cue violin),

But this small dog
does not fit in.

"It's true," she sniffs, "I've tried my best,
But I'm not made like all the rest.

And that's why I've made up my mind
To leave this town, my home, behind."

On
her
own
and
out of
place,

She
sighs
a sigh
and
packs
her
case.

Through winter...

Springtime...

Summer...

Fall...

From ocean deep...

...to mountain tall.

She walks 'til she can walk no more.
Is this the place she's looking for?

"Well bless my bow-wow, can it be?
A hundred others just like me!

But wait. Look closer. Can you see
One dog behaving differently?

Somebody this
afternoon

Is whistling a
different tune.

Here's something she knows all about:
A classic case of 'Odd Dog Out'.

"Poor thing," she says, "I feel for you.
I once was an outsider too."

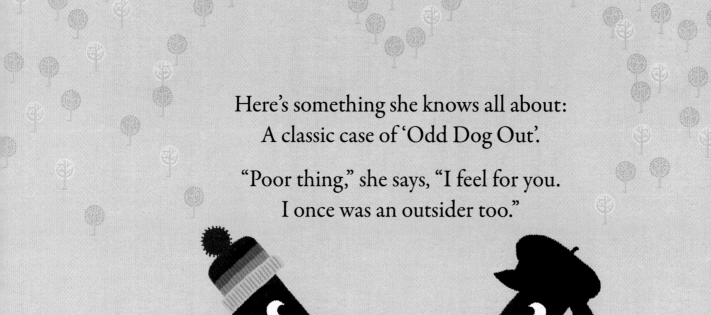

"Oh, not at all. You've got it wrong.
I really feel like I belong.

I love to stand out from the crowd!
And so should you. Stand tall. Be proud."

Her tummy flips,
Her belly flops,
As finally
the penny drops.

"That dog is right.
It's plain to see
There's nothing wrong
with being me."

Her little tail
begins to wag.
She smiles a smile
and grabs her bag.

"I'm sorry but I have to fly."

"Good luck my friend!"

They wave goodbye.

From night and moon to light and sun. Her journey home has just begun.

For busy dogs
a busy day.

But look who's back!
Hip hip hooray!

They cheer! They clap! They whoop! They shout!
"We've really missed our Odd Dog Out!

You've made us all appreciate
That being different's really great!"

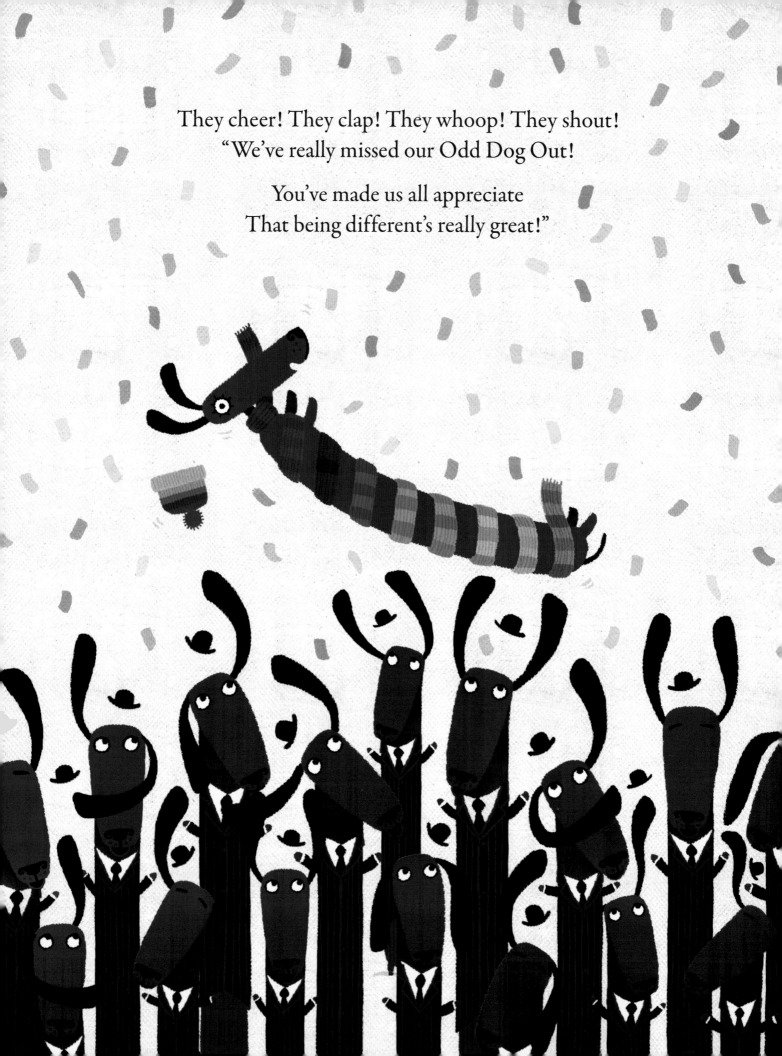

It's true! Look closer. Can you see
More dogs behaving differently?

Each one a doggy superstar...

So blaze a trail.

Be who *you* are.